The Aggressor

By

Jeffrey A. James

Merriam-Webster define aggressor as "one that commits or practices aggression."

Do you feel as if you are not enjoying all the financial benefits of being a believer? Have you ever felt like the things you have prayed for were blocked or are being held up? If you answered yes, then this book is for you. I believe you will find the answer to your question in this small yet helpful and informative book.

Many people like yourself are going through life wondering why they pray for financial help, but it never seems to come. Prayerfully after reading this book you will have one of the missing keys to unlock the financial future that God ordained for you to have and enjoy. This is not a book that's written to encourage you to give more. Even though you can't go wrong if you do. But this is a book to help you receive from what you have already given.

If you are like me, results oriented, then you are always exploring ways to get the max out of what you have done. This book will open up a new way of looking at what I believe to be one the believers' favorite passage of scripture.

I hear people quoting, singing, and telling others about this scripture all the time. It's also one the most quoted scriptures that Pastors use during offering. The other is of course Malachi 3:8-10. Which I believe to **some**, is the most dreaded scripture in the Bible. Why? Because of error on the part of Pastors, Ministers, and lay people. But that's for another book.

The scripture I'm referring to is Luke 6:38. Open your heart and mind and receive revelation on how to use this missing key and receive the financial abundance that God promised you.

Get ready to unlock the door to your financial abundance so you can leave an inheritance for generations to come.

Luke 6:38

Give, and it shall be given unto you; good measure, pressed down, and shaken together, and running over, shall men give into your bosom. For with the same measure that ye mete withal it shall be measured to you again.

This is one of the most quoted scriptures used by people when they give in expectation. I have quoted this scripture so much that it's permanently embedded in my mind and heart. I often confess this as I go throughout my day. I may be washing my car, working in the yard, or driving somewhere, it really doesn't matter, this scripture just comes out of my mouth without me focusing on it.

I've found that many people love this scripture because it offers hope when they give. It takes the sting away from releasing their precious seed, by believing that their gift will be returned good measure, pressed down, shaken together, and running over. Immediately after giving the seed, they begin speaking to the seed to return as the scripture declares. After all the Bible does say in *Job 22:28 "Thou shalt also decree a thing, and it shall be established unto thee: and the light shall shine upon thy ways."*

Mark 11:22-24 says "And Jesus answering saith unto them, Have faith in God. 23 For verily I say unto you, That whosoever shall say unto this mountain, Be thou removed, and be thou cast into the sea; and shall not doubt in his heart, but shall believe that those things which he saith shall come to pass; he shall have whatsoever he saith. 24 Therefore I say unto you, What things soever ye desire, when ye pray, believe that ye receive them, and ye shall have them."

Therefore, there are scriptural references for speaking and decreeing things that causes manifestation. I am a firm believer in declaring, decreeing, and speaking the Word of God with expectation that I will receive what I say.

Proverbs 18:21 says "Death and life are in the power of the tongue: and they that love it shall eat the fruit thereof." Therefore, we should speak to our seed and declare what the Word says we can have.

But let's go back to *Luke 6:38 "Give, and it shall be given unto you; good measure, pressed down, and shaken together, and running over, shall men give into your bosom. For with the same measure that ye mete withal it shall be measured to you again."*

Let me encourage you to continue declaring; give, and it shall be given unto you; good measure, pressed down, and shaken together, and running over, and don't be passive about it.

Become The Aggressor!

You may be asking how do I become the aggressor? You become the aggressor by not only speaking to your seed, but also speaking to, praying for, and declaring prosperity over the men that God instructs to give unto you.

We often forget the part of **Luke 6:38 that says** "*...shall men give into your bosom.*" If men are to give into my bosom, then I want those men blessed, safe, prosperous, wealthy, healthy, giving, obedient, generous, cheerful, sensitive to God, and loving. I also want their family blessed and healthy, and their job and/or business to be successful. So, in my prayer time and whenever I think about it, I should become aggressive about declaring, decreeing, and speaking these things over their lives.

Become the aggressor by rebuking Satan and rendering him ineffective against these men. Take authority over any financial, physical, spiritual, relational, or emotional attacks that Satan may try to use to hinder them from obeying God and giving into your bosom.

Elijah the Tishbite was a man of God who gave himself fully to the ministry. (Side note) When we give ourselves fully to the ministry of the Gospel, God causes the sustaining resources we need to be manifested.

And Elijah the Tishbite, who was of the inhabitants of Gilead, said unto Ahab, As the LORD God of Israel liveth, before whom I stand, there shall not be dew nor rain these years, but according to my word. 2 And the word of the LORD came unto him, saying, 3 Get thee hence, and turn thee eastward, and hide thyself by the brook Cherith, that is before Jordan. 4 And it shall be, that thou shalt drink of the brook; and I have commanded the ravens to feed thee there. 5 So he went and did according unto the word of the LORD: for he went and dwelt by the brook Cherith, that is before Jordan. 6 And the ravens brought him bread and flesh in the morning, and bread and flesh in the evening; and he drank of the brook. 7 And it came to pass after a while, that the brook dried up, because there had been no rain in the land. I Kings 17:1

God commanded the ravens to feed Elijah! I don't know about you, and I don't know if he did, but if I was Elijah, I would have been praying for and speaking well over those ravens. I would have been declaring that they obey God, arrive safely and do exactly what He commanded them to do.

Let's look further into **I Kings 17.**

8 And the word of the LORD came unto him, saying, 9 Arise, get thee to Zarephath, which belongeth to Zidon, and dwell there: behold, I have commanded a widow woman there to sustain thee.

Here we see God instructs Elijah to move from the dried-up brook and go to Zarephath where He had commanded a widow woman there to sustain him.

I like to look at this passage as God taking Elijah out of one place and into another. Believe it or not, God does the same thing with us. He takes us out of one place in life into another. He takes us out of one financial situation into a better one. Initially it may not appear better, but if all parties obey God, things will be better for everyone involved.

God says to Elijah in verse 9, *"Arise, get thee to Zarephath, which belongeth to Zidon, and dwell there:*

*behold, I have commanded a widow woman there to **sustain thee**."*

Three things you can expect from God when He takes you out and into:

1. **God will give you strength to sustain.** I like to call it "**sustaining strength**." Sustaining strength is strength that supports and maintain you physically and mentally so you continue your journey. Once God brings you out, He gives you strength to endure. He gives you strength to endure until you secure.

2. **God gives you strength to secure.** Once you learn to endure, God gives you sustaining and securing strength so you can secure your place, position, and possessions. God doesn't just want you to see what He has for you; He wants you to have it and enjoy it. He wants you to have and enjoy that place, position, and the possessions. According to scripture, He gives us richly all things to enjoy.

3. **God gives you strength for success.** Success doesn't come without a price. If you are willing to pay that price, God will give you the strength you need to become successful in your endeavors. Many people put everything they got into becoming successful, but when they finally are, they are too worn out to enjoy it. When I say God gives you strength for success, I am referring to strength to become successful, maintain it, and enjoy it.

Again, God says to Elijah in verse 9, *"Arise, get thee to Zarephath, which belongeth to Zidon, and dwell there: behold, I have commanded a widow woman there to sustain thee."*

Now let's look at this from all three perspectives: God, The Widow Woman, and Elijah.

God already knew the end result. He knew what He was going to do. He knew everyone's financial, emotional, spiritual, and physical condition. He knew what they needed and had a plan to get them out of their present situation into a better one. He was just waiting on the two of them to line up and obey. God told the Widow Woman to sustain Elijah before he arrived. Because Elijah was a giver and gave himself fully to God and the ministry, God made provision for him before he needed it.

This is God's mode of operation for believers who are aggressive in giving and obeying Him. He makes provision for us before the need arises. That's why it's important to give and speak blessings over the people who God will use to give to you. You don't have to know who they are, but know that God's Word is true and that He has commanded men to give to you. Knowing this gives you confidence when you give and when you are expecting to receive.

The Widow Woman was commanded by God to take care of Elijah. Therefore, God had to give her sustaining strength to endure until he arrived. I don't believe she fully understood that God was sustaining her so she could be used to sustain Elijah. Sustain means to maintain and make provision. God was instructing the Widow Woman to maintain and make provision for Elijah. When God spoke to her, He knew her financial situation and He also knew that if she would tap into His sustaining and securing strength, things would turn around for her. Many believers are in the same situation she was in; not having enough to spare, but are being instructed to give to or sustain someone else. We don't know if the Widow Woman prayed that Elijah would arrive quickly and safely or if she knew that God was going to use him to change her life. But one thing we need to understand is that if God told you to give or sustain someone and you are in need, He has plans on turning your financial situation around. So instead of focusing on what you don't have, begin to speak blessings, safety, and prosperity over the person or place that God is instructing you to give to. This is how you become aggressive in receiving. The Widow Woman was able to secure her and her son's future success by obeying God and making provision for Elijah.

1Kings 17:13 And Elijah said unto her, Fear not; go and do as thou hast said: but make me thereof a little cake first, and bring it unto me, and after make for thee and for thy son. 14 For thus saith the LORD God of Israel, The barrel of meal shall not waste, neither shall the cruse of oil fail, until the day that the LORD sendeth rain upon the earth. <u>15 And she went and did according to the saying of Elijah: and she, and he, and her house, did eat many days. 16 And the barrel of meal wasted not, neither did the cruse of oil fail, according to the word of the LORD, which he spake by Elijah.</u>

Elijah was instructed by God to leave out one place and go into another. I said it earlier, but it bears repeating again. If God takes you out of a place, then He will give you strength to sustain, secure, and also strength for success in the new place. Just like us, Elijah had to trust God as a provider and protector even though he couldn't see what was in store for him.

God sustained Elijah with food from ravens and water from the brook of Cherith. But when the brook dries up, God instructs him to go to Zarephath where a widow woman would sustain him. Even though Elijah had a Word from God, it would still be beneficial for him if he prayed for and spoke well over the woman who God was going to use to sustain him. Likewise, if God has prepared the heart of men and women to give into our bosoms, it would be beneficial for us to pray for them and to speak well over them and their family. There are times when God speaks to the heart of men to give to us, but Satan gets involved and attacks them to keep them from obeying God and blessing us. For this reason, some of your prayers seem to go unanswered when it comes to finances. They may have been answered, but Satan intervened and attacked the giver which caused what you needed to be delayed. Become the aggressor and take authority over Satan and his schemes by speaking the Word of God over the people whom God has commanded to give, help, and sustain you. Also understand that you are the giver in Luke 6:38 as well. Therefore, it is imperative that you continue to speak well over your finances, family, business, jobs, and endeavors.

Godly Decisions Produce Godly Results

Becoming the aggressor is a Godly decision, based on a Godly principle. Whenever we decide to do what the Word instructs us, we can expect what the Word promises us. You've made a decision to give, now make the decision to receive just as Luke 6:38 declares. *"Give, <u>and it shall be given unto you; good measure, pressed down, and shaken together, and running over, shall men give into your bosom.</u> For with the same measure that ye mete withal it shall be measured to you again."* In my book "Leadership Seeing and Seizing the Opportunity," I share some insightful information pertaining to decisions. Here's an excerpt from Chapter 6: Don't Play with Snakes, They Can be Deadly.

We are forced to make decisions every day. Some are difficult and others are easy. Our decisions are like roads, some are smooth, bumpy, long, short, and some rocky. Regardless of the type of road you are on, there's one thing they have in common, they all are leading you somewhere. It may lead to a place you didn't desire to go but ended up there. Like roads, every decision we make is leading us somewhere. We may not like where they take us, but the outcome was based on a decision we made. Some of our decisions are smooth and short, we don't have to think about them much or get any advice. They just flow right along with life. Others are long, bumpy, rough and uncomfortable. You feel these decisions as you are making them. You experience pain and discomfort as you make the decision, knowing the outcome may be just as bad or worse than the decision-making process itself. These are the decisions that determine your level of success. Most of the time, it's not the easy, smooth decisions that determine your success. If it were, everyone would be successful in every endeavor. It's when you are faced with the long, hard, rocky, rough, and uncomfortable decision that you pass the test of leadership. Making the right decision when it's hard is what makes you a powerful, successful leader. Great leaders make decisions that could cost them their existence in the organization or even their lives. The decisions that cost you the most, usually gives you the greatest return. The more challenging the decision, the more gratifying the reward. In leadership, the decision you fear the most may be the one that rewards you the best.

Eight things to remember when a decision must be made:

1. *Pray before you make the decision and ask for wisdom.*
2. *When you make the decision, make it based on Godly principles.*
3. *Get understanding about whatever you are dealing with.*
4. *Make sure your priorities are in order and your heart is right before making the decision.*
5. *Believe God for the desired results.*
6. *Make up your mind that you can handle the outcome.*
7. *If you begin to see things that appear contrary to your desired results, don't cave in and give up. Speak*

the desired results and thank God as if your desired results have already manifested.

8. Walk by faith and not by fear.

Don't ever make a decision that needs God's attention without consulting Him first. It's not wise to make the decision and then pray and ask God to bless it. By doing this, you could be asking God to bless a decision that He didn't want you to make. If God didn't want you to make the decision you made, why would He bless it? Wise leaders ask God first, and then proceed with His desires.

James 1:5

If any of you lack wisdom, let him ask of God, that giveth to all men liberally, and upbraideth not; and it shall be given him.

All decisions should be based upon Godly principles. If your decisions are based on Godly principles, your outcome will resemble Godly results. I don't want to give you the impression that just because your decision is based on Godly principles that they will always generate the results you *desire. They may not produce your desire results, but more times than not, they will resemble Godly results. In other words, even when you don't get the results you desired, you may still have peace that everything will work together for your good. Also, what you desired may not have been God's best for you; therefore, He made adjustments for you so things would work out better and in your favor. Sometimes when things don't turn out the way we desire them to, we get discouraged and forget to ask God for His assistance. Other times we may need to wait on God and have some patience. Godly results can take more time than fleshly results when others are involved. For some things to work out, the heart of several people may need to change. Unfortunately, we don't know how many people need a change of heart, how many people have a part to play in the decision, and who those people are. We may not have these answers, neither do we need to know them because the heart of the king is in the hand of God and He turns it whichever way He wills.*

Wow! Did you get that? For some things to work out, the heart of several people may need to change.

That's why we should intervene spiritually for all the people who God instructs to give to us. As stated above, we don't know how many people need a change of heart, how many people have a part to play in the decision, and who those people are. We may not have these answers, neither do we need to know them because the heart of the king is in the hand of God and He turns it whichever way He wills. Our job is to speak life to them, declare God's blessing over them, and pray for them and their family's well-being. We don't have to know who they are to make a quality decision to pray and declare God's best for them. You've made the decision to give, now make the decision to aggressively declare God's blessings over the givers.

The Real Test Comes After the Lesson

Luke 5:1 And it came to pass, that, as the people pressed upon him to hear the word of God, he stood by the lake of Gennesaret, 2 And saw two ships standing by the lake: but the fishermen were gone out of them, and were washing their nets. 3 And he entered into one of the ships, which was Simon's, and prayed him that he would thrust out a little from the land. And he sat down, and taught the people out of the ship.

Verse 3 says Jesus taught the people out of the ship. I would imagine that faith and obedience was an essential part of Jesus' teaching. I came to that conclusion based on the scriptures that follow verse 3. Jesus taught the lesson, now comes the test.

4 Now when he had left speaking, he said unto Simon, (Here's the test) Launch out into the deep, and let down your nets for a draught. 5 And Simon answering said unto him, Master, we have toiled all the night, and have taken nothing: nevertheless at thy word I will let down the net. 6 And when they had this done, they inclosed a great multitude of fishes: and their net brake. 7 And they beckoned unto their partners, which were in the other ship, that they should come and help them. And they came, and filled both the ships, so that they began to sink.

21

After fishing all night only to end with empty nets is devastating to fishermen. But after Jesus' lesson, Peter was faced with a test. But this time he had a Word from the Lord. One Word from the Lord can change your life forever!

Peter went fishing the first time, but the second time he didn't go fishing, he went **OBEYING**! Anytime you go obeying, you are not going in your own power and wisdom, you are going in God's power and wisdom because He sent you.

The first time Peter went fishing, he caught nothing because it was based on knowledge and skill, but the second time he caught an abundance of fish because he went based on obedience to the Word. This was a faith lesson for Peter and those who were with him. Peter had the "this time it's on you Lord attitude," which is the exact attitude Jesus wanted him to have. Because Jesus told him to do it, Jesus became responsible to manifest the fish. Jesus knew if Peter obeyed, He'd produce the results.

When you obey God, the results are not on your shoulders, but on God's!

Always remember this: Your obedience in small matters creates supernatural abundance and overflow!

I encourage you to "**Go Obeying" because the real test comes after the lesson.**

The Violent Take it by Force!

Matthew 11:12 And from the days of John the Baptist until now the kingdom of heaven suffereth violence, and the violent take it by force.

Don't sit and wait for the enemy to get involved. Be the aggressor and attack him before he attacks. Use the Word of God to keep him at bay. In Chapter 9 of my book How to Defeat Life's Giants, I write on how David successfully defeated Goliath. I gave several key points that helped David successfully defeat Goliath:

❖ David was proactive and not reactive.

❖ David didn't allow Goliath to attack him, but he ran towards him and used the tools that God had blessed him with.

❖ The battle was already David's, but he had to be aggressive and use what God had already given him and not wait for God to release some special anointing for fighting a giant.

❖ David had all the anointing he needed. His job was to attack the enemy before the enemy attacked him.

David defeated Goliath by attacking him first. He didn't wait to fight off Goliath's attack, he pursued and attacked him. This is the attitude we must always have towards the enemy.

The Violent take it by Force!

Violent in Matthew 11:12 means a forcer and energetic. It could read like this "and the energetic forcer or enforcer take it by force."

Become violent (**energetic enforcer**) with receiving. No longer being lackadaisical about receiving. Become energetic and enforce the Word of God by speaking to and praying for the men that are ordained by God to be a blessing to you.

This process is not just for those in need, it's also for those who are doing well financially. Luke 6:38 **doesn't** say Give, and it shall be given unto you; good measure, pressed down, and shaken together, and running over, shall men give into your bosom **when you are in need**. For with the same measure that ye mete withal it shall be measured to you again. It says *"Give, and it shall be given unto you; good measure, pressed down, and shaken together, and running over, shall men give into your bosom. For with the same measure that ye mete withal it shall be measured to you again."* The only prerequisite for men giving into your bosom is that you give first regardless of your financial status. Therefore, we all need to become energetic enforcers concerning our giving. I honestly believe this is a missing link to a greater level of financial prosperity.

2 Corinthian 4:13

We having the same spirit of faith, according as it is written, I believed, and therefore have I spoken; we also believe, and therefore speak;

Based on scripture, I believe men are supposed to give into my bosom as well as I am to give into their bosom. Being that I believe it, I speak it and speak to them. I become a barrier between them and the evil one who comes to steal, kill, and destroy. I become a barrier to protect their finances and their wellbeing. I refuse to allow Satan to successfully attack the people whom God has ordained to give into my bosom whether it's spiritually or financially. My Supply Warehouse doors are open for receiving and my Distribution Warehouse doors are open and I continually distribute.

Galatians 6:7 Be not deceived; God is not mocked: for whatsoever a man soweth, that shall he also reap.

Increase your giving so you can increase your receiving! Get aggressive about giving and receiving, and don't forget to also be aggressive by rebuking Satan and rendering him ineffective against the men God has commanded to give into your bosom.

In your prayer time and whenever you think about it, become aggressive about declaring, decreeing, and speaking over the lives of the men God has commanded to give to you. Call them blessed, safe, prosperous, wealthy, healthy, giving, obedient, generous, cheerful, sensitive to God, and loving. Also declare that their families are blessed and healthy, and their job and/or businesses are successful.

FROM THIS DAY FORWARD
BE THE AGGRESSOR!

Psalms 66:12 Thou hast caused men to ride over our heads; we went through fire and through water: but thou broughtest us out into a wealthy place.

Get ready to move into your wealthy place!